SNOWED IN WITH GRUMPY

EM TATE

Chapter 1

Addy

The snow's falling heavily, blanketing the world in a pristine coat of white. I squint through the frosted windshield, struggling to see the road ahead as flakes continue to swirl and settle. The icy chill penetrates the interior of my car, even though I've cranked the heat to its highest setting. My breath fogs up the glass, adding to the already thick layer of frost that's spreading like a delicate, frosty spiderweb across the glass.

Every few minutes, I swipe at the condensation with the edge of my glove, but it feels like an endless battle against the relentless snowstorm. My knuckles are white from gripping the steering wheel, and my heartbeat quickens with every skid and slide on the slippery road. This cross-country drive to visit my parents for the holidays is quickly turning into the worst decision I've ever made. The snow, once magical and serene, now seems like an unforgiving obstacle course that threatens to swallow me whole.

My car sputters and wheezes, each jolt sending a fresh wave of anxiety through me. I chew nervously on my bottom lip, my breath coming in short, shaky bursts as I grip the steering wheel tighter. The engine's labored groan is punctuated by occasional, desperate coughs that seem to echo my growing panic. I pray for a miracle, for the engine to catch its second wind and propel me through this winter wasteland.

But my prayers go unanswered. With a final shuddering gasp, the car succumbs to the relentless cold and dies, its engine giving up in a cloud of exhaust that quickly dissipates into the snowy night. The car rolls to a stop, its once vibrant engine now reduced to a silent, lifeless heap. I stare out at the road stretching endlessly in both directions, a seemingly infinite expanse of snow and darkness, stretching for miles in every direction. The isolation and hopelessness of the scene mirror my own feelings as I sit in the frigid, quiet car, feeling the weight of my poor decision settle heavily on my shoulders.

I reach for my phone from its resting place on the passenger seat, but it feels just like my car—dead and unresponsive. The screen remains dark despite my frantic swipes and taps. A sinking feeling of despair settles in my stomach. No. No, no, no. This can't be happening.

The night is deep and the snow continues to fall relentlessly, creating an eerie stillness that amplifies my anxiety. It's been over an hour since I last saw a single car pass by, and the silence is oppressive. The road is deserted, stretching out in an endless sea of white, and I realize with growing dread that I might be stranded here, alone and exposed to the cold.

The cold is seeping into the car, despite the heater's

feeble attempts to fend it off. I shiver uncontrollably, imagining the harsh reality of spending the night in this frigid isolation. My heart pounds rapidly in my chest, each beat a reminder of my worsening predicament. My bottom lip is nearly chewed to shreds from my anxious nibbling as I try to focus on a potential solution, desperately clinging to the hope that someone will come by soon or that I'll somehow find a way out of this nightmarish situation.

A sudden, sharp tap on my windshield jerks me out of my mounting panic. I whip my head toward the driver's side window, straining to make out any details through the frosted glass. The outline of a figure becomes clearer as I fumble to open the car door, the biting cold air immediately hitting my face with a stinging, icy intensity.

Standing there, towering over me, is a man whose dark eyes seem to pierce through the dim light. He has an air of rugged charm, with a face weathered by the elements and a rough, mountain-man look that somehow exudes both strength and kindness.

As I scramble out of the car, my movements are frantic and unsteady. I nearly spill out of the vehicle in my haste to reach him. I throw my arms around his neck, pulling him into a tight embrace. My emotions overwhelm me, and I can barely control the sobs that escape me. "You saved me," I choke out, my voice trembling with relief and gratitude as I cling to him, the warmth of his body providing a stark, comforting contrast to the harsh cold that enveloped me moments before.

I pull away from the embrace, a sudden wave of caution washing over me. The realization hits that this is a stranger, and my initial relief might have been misplaced. For all I know, he could be here with intentions far more sinister than rescuing me. I quickly step back, pressing my back against the car for support as I struggle to regain some composure. "I'm sorry," I stammer, my teeth chattering from the biting cold.

The man's voice is rough, cutting through the frigid air. "What are you doing out here?"

"My car broke down," I explain, my voice shaky. "I'm trying to make it to Florida to visit my parents."

He gives me a pointed look, his breath visible in the frosty air. "You're a long way from Florida."

I let out a weary sigh, the reality of my situation sinking in. "I know."

The man's expression softens slightly, but his tone remains serious. "You're going to freeze to death out here."

Another resigned sigh escapes me. "I know."

He studies me intently, as if searching for some hidden reason behind my predicament, his eyes narrowed with suspicion. Crossing his arms over his broad chest, he stands there, his posture a mix of skepticism and irritation. The cold seems to deepen the furrows in his brow, and his rugged demeanor only adds to the tension.

I can feel my frustration bubbling up. I huff out a breath, the icy air mingling with the heat of my exasperation. "Are you going to help me, or what?" I snap, my voice edged with a blend of cold and annoyance.

The corner of his lip twitches, just the slightest curve upward, as if he's on the verge of a smile. The small, fleeting expression softens his otherwise stern features, hinting at a trace of amusement or perhaps even reluctant empathy. "There's a storm moving in. You'll have to stay with me," he says, his voice steady despite the wind howling around us.

I glance around, my breath forming visible puffs in the frigid air. The surrounding landscape is an unending expanse of snow, and I can't see any signs of civilization no house, no cabin, nothing but the white blur of the storm. "Where's that?" I ask, my voice tinged with confusion and hope.

He points toward a snowy hilltop, barely visible through the swirling snow. "Just up the mountain a bit."

I look up at the daunting slope, feeling a wave of uncertainty. The thought of hiking in this weather seems nearly impossible. "What are you doing out this far from home anyway?" I ask, trying to distract myself from the growing anxiety.

His expression softens just a bit, and a small, almost mischievous smile tugs at the corner of his lips. "Hunting."

I raise an eyebrow, incredulous. "In the dark? In a snowstorm?" I begin to move around my car, opening the trunk and grabbing my bags with clumsy, frostbitten fingers.

"Not that type of hunting," he replies cryptically, his vague answer doing little to ease my apprehension. The snow continues to fall heavily, and I can't help but feel a growing unease about this entire situation.

He steps in to help me with my bags, his movements efficient and confident despite the worsening weather. Once he's finished securing my car as best as he can in these conditions, he gestures towards the side of the road. "This way," he says, his voice cutting through the blizzard as he leads me toward a snowmobile that's parked nearby, its engine rumbling softly in the storm.

"We're going to ride on that?" I ask, eyeing the snowmobile with a mix of relief and trepidation.

He chuckles softly, the sound almost lost to the howling wind. "How else do you expect to get up there?"

I can't help but feel a bit sheepish. "I guess I hadn't thought of that." Honestly, I'd been bracing myself for a grueling hike up the snow-covered hill, picturing myself freezing to death halfway up. The prospect of the snowmobile is a welcome relief.

After we position my bags securely on the rack at the back of the snowmobile, he mounts it with practiced ease, then pats the spot behind him. "Hop on," he instructs, his tone leaving no room for hesitation.

I blink, momentarily stunned by the proximity of his invitation. "Right," I say, trying my best to mount the snowmobile gracefully and avoid brushing against the handsome stranger more than necessary. As I settle behind him, I feel a rush of cold air and the warmth of his body just inches away, amplifying my mixed feelings of anxiety and gratitude.

"Hold on tight," he says, revving the engine to life, and instinctively my arms fly around his waist, gripping onto him tightly.

This is definitely not how I saw my Christmas vacation going.

Chapter 2

Travis

I don't trust Mayfair, and I definitely don't trust Dennis Mayfair to come up with something like this—especially not on Christmas. It wouldn't surprise me if the old man hired a pretty brunette in need of rescuing, setting her up to spy on me and get the inside scoop on whatever I'm planning.

As the snowmobile roars to life, I feel her arms wrap around me, and it catches me off guard. It's been a long time since I've had a woman's touch—years of working hard and keeping my guard up have left little room for anything personal. Her warmth against my back is a stark reminder of how isolated I've been. I've been so consumed with my own schemes and distrust that I haven't allowed myself a moment of vulnerability. Her unexpected closeness stirs something inside me, a blend of surprise and an old, almost forgotten sense of connection.

"My name's Addy," she calls out, her voice barely audible over the growing roar of the wind and the snowmobile's engine.

"Travis," I reply, though I suspect she's already heard that or pieced it together from my earlier mention. Her arms tighten around me slightly as we move, the touch a strange but not entirely unwelcome distraction.

I guide the snowmobile up the mountain, the snow now coming down in heavy, relentless sheets. The path ahead becomes increasingly obscured by the blizzard, but the faint outline of my cabin soon comes into view, a welcome beacon of shelter amidst the storm. I steer the snowmobile right up to the front porch, the vehicle sliding smoothly to a halt in the snow.

Addy dismounts first, her movements careful as she steps onto the snowy ground. I follow, immediately beginning to unload her bags. The snow is falling harder now, creating a thick, fluffy carpet on the porch and blurring the edges of the cabin's warm, inviting light. I help her carry the bags inside, the warmth of the cabin a stark contrast to the cold bite of the storm outside. As we step through the door, the cozy interior of the cabin wraps around us like a comforting embrace, the fire crackling softly in the hearth and promising much-needed warmth.

"Wow," Addy breathes out, her eyes widening as she takes in the cozy, inviting interior of the cabin. "This place is so warm and nice." Her raised eyebrow suggests surprise, as if she hadn't expected me to have such a comfortable retreat.

I nod, trying to hide a small smile at her reaction. "Let's get you warmed up and unpacked," I say, gesturing toward the inviting warmth of the cabin. "Hopefully the storm will have passed by morning, and I can get your car fixed so you can continue on to Florida."

Her smile brightens the room, casting a warm glow that seems to permeate every corner of the cabin. It's captivating, and I find myself momentarily mesmerized by her presence. "Thank you," she whispers, her voice soft and genuine as she takes one last appreciative look around the cabin, her gaze lingering on the fire crackling in the hearth and the soft glow of the lights.

"You hungry?" I ask, breaking the spell and shifting my focus to the practicalities of the situation.

She blinks, her expression a mix of relief and hesitation. "I hate to impose," she begins, her voice tinged with exhaustion, "but yes, I'm starving. I was hoping to reach a little town soon so I could pull over and find a quick bite."

I study her carefully, my skepticism resurfacing. Could she really be a spy hired by Mayfair? I try to gauge her sincerity as I respond, "Snowflake Village is about twenty miles up the road." I move toward the kitchen, the warm, inviting aroma of the cabin's interior contrasting sharply with the bitter cold outside. "Lucky for you, I'm completely stocked up."

Addy's eyes light up with a hint of surprise, and she stutters slightly as she offers, "I can make us dinner...as a thank you." Her offer catches me off guard.

A corporate spy offering to cook? It seems unlikely, but the thought crosses my mind. Maybe she wants full access to my kitchen, or perhaps she thinks I might be hiding sensitive documents in the fridge.

I consider her offer, a wry smile playing at the corners of my mouth. "I can cook," I reply firmly, my tone leaving no room for argument. "You don't need to worry about it. Let's just get you settled, and we can figure out dinner later."

"I really appreciate this, Travis," she says, her voice soft with genuine gratitude.

As she stands in the warm glow of the cabin's light, I can't help but notice just how pretty she is. Her features are striking—big, expressive amber-colored eyes that shimmer with sincerity, and a warm, inviting smile that lights up her face. Her brown hair is tousled from the snow and wind, framing her face in loose waves that add to her natural charm.

Mayfair clearly didn't hold back when selecting her for this scheme. Despite my lingering doubts, it's hard to ignore how her presence adds a touch of warmth and beauty to the otherwise stark setting of the cabin.

Chapter 3

Addy

The storm outside howls relentlessly, its fierce gusts causing the cabin to tremble with each blast. I shudder as I think about what might have happened had Travis not shown up when he did. The icy wind and driving snow would have left me stranded in the cold, with no clear path to safety.

It seems like sheer luck that he arrived at the right time and the right place. I'm profoundly grateful for his unexpected rescue. It's why I offered to cook dinner as a gesture of thanks, though he firmly insisted on handling it himself.

"Where's the restroom?" I ask him, trying to focus on something practical.

He gestures down a long hallway, his finger pointing toward the end. "First door on the left."

I give him a grateful smile before heading in that direction. As soon as I step into the bathroom, the warmth and privacy are a welcome relief from the storm's fury. I pull out my dead phone, its screen dark and unresponsive. Knowing I need to get it charged so I can update my parents on my whereabouts and let them know I'm on my way, I scan the room for an outlet. The storm's howls outside serve as a constant reminder of how precarious my situation was, making me even more determined to get in touch with my family as soon as possible.

I plug my phone into the outlet, relieved to see the charging icon light up on the screen. Then, I move toward the sink and splash some warm water over my face. The comforting warmth of the water contrasts sharply with the freezing cold I've been enduring. I take a deep breath, letting the soothing sensation wash away some of my anxiety.

Things could definitely be worse, I remind myself. Here I am, stuck in a cozy cabin with a stunning man, and he's cooking dinner for us. It's a far better scenario than being stranded in the snowstorm, and the prospect of a warm meal and a safe haven feels like a small miracle.

Feeling a bit more optimistic, I leave the bathroom and make my way back to the main room. I inform Travis that my phone is charging, and I'll be able to alert my parents and let them know where I am.

He nods, his attention focused on the kitchen where he's busy preparing something that smells incredibly inviting. The aroma drifts through the cabin, mixing with the warmth from the crackling fire.

"Need any help?" I ask, my voice hopeful.

He shakes his head with a faint smile. "Nope. Just sit by the fire and relax."

I take his advice, settling into a comfortable spot near the fireplace. The warmth of the flames and the scent of the meal in progress make me feel more at ease. For now, I let myself unwind, grateful for the unexpected turn of events that brought me to this cozy sanctuary.

"What is it you do for work?" Travis calls from the kitchen, his voice carrying over the soft crackle of the fire and the sizzling sounds coming from the stove.

I raise an eyebrow, sensing an odd note in his small talk. "I own a little bakery. It's called Addy's Sweet Treats. What about you?"

He nods as he stirs a giant pot of pasta sauce, the rich aroma wafting through the cabin and making my stomach rumble in anticipation. His concentration is evident as he stirs, and then he raises his hand, his pointer finger wagging at me in a mock-serious manner. "Oh no you don't."

I give him a puzzled look, a smile tugging at my lips as I try to interpret his reaction. "Okay," I say, wondering if he's simply not in the mood for discussing his work. Maybe he's a recluse, living in this remote mountain cabin to escape from the complexities of a busy life.

He shifts his focus back to the pot and fires off his next question, seemingly eager to turn the conversation. "Where do you live?"

"Cresthaven," I reply, my voice carrying back to him. "About an hour from here."

His curiosity seems piqued, though he remains focused on the task at hand. The pasta sauce continues to simmer, filling the cabin with its mouthwatering scent, and I can't help but feel a bit more at ease, despite the strange circumstances that brought me here. "The bakery's in Cresthaven?"

I nod, wondering what on earth kind of question is that. Of course it is. "Yes," I say.

"Dinner's almost ready. I'm not sure if you'll get any

signal up here, but you can see if your phone is charged enough to make a call."

I get up from my comfy chair. "Thank you," I say as I head off back toward the bathroom, wanting desperately to let my parents know I'm okay.

If even the man I'm with is asking me strange questions.

It's almost as if he doesn't trust me, and who knows, maybe he thinks I might be the serial killer.

For the record, I'm not.

Or am I?

Just kidding, I get squeamish at the sight of blood.

Chapter 4

Travis

As Addy disappears back into the bathroom, I pull out my own cell phone and dial my brother, Jackson. The pasta sauce is simmering nicely, but I can't shake the feeling that something about this situation doesn't quite add up.

"Hey, what do you know about corporate spies?" I ask him, trying to keep my tone casual as he answers the call, sounding slightly groggy.

"Like double-oh-seven stuff?" Jackson replies, his voice tinged with amusement.

"Sure," I say, stirring the pot of pasta sauce with a wooden spoon to keep it from sticking and burning. The rich, savory aroma fills the kitchen, but my mind is preoccupied with thoughts of Addy and her unexpected arrival.

Jackson chuckles on the other end of the line. "Why?"

I quickly tell him the situation, explaining how she showed up out of nowhere. Right on the very night we received the message from Mayfair's men, saying they had a surprise for us. It's why I went hunting around my property, to make sure everything was safe.

Mayfair's had eyes on my inventions for years. They've tried to weasel their way into my company before, and I wouldn't put it past them to concoct an idea this absurd.

Jackson interrupts my wandering thoughts. "You think she's a spy?"

"I don't know," I admit, my eyes flicking toward the hallway where Addy is. "She's just a little too convenient, showing up right when I was about to head up the mountain. And she's awfully pretty for someone who's supposed to be a threat."

Jackson's laughter fades into a thoughtful hum. "Well, if she's here to spy, she's certainly got the cover story down pat. But if she's genuine, you might want to give her the benefit of the doubt."

I nod to myself, even though he can't see me. "Yeah, I guess. I'll keep my guard up but try to be polite. Thanks for the insight."

As I hang up, I return my attention to the kitchen. The pasta sauce is nearly ready, and the rich scent is beginning to blend with the comforting aroma of the cabin. My thoughts keep drifting back to Addy and her mysterious charm, and I can't help but wonder what other secrets she might be hiding.

She comes out of the bathroom with a smile, her face looking a little more relaxed than earlier. "I was able to get ahold of my parents. They told me the storm's only getting worse. I tried downloading a weather app on my phone, but I didn't have enough juice," she explains, her voice tinged with a mix of concern and lingering hope.

I nod and grab my phone from the counter, pulling up the local weather app, hoping maybe she's wrong. As she screen loads, I see the forecast, and it's grim. Snow. Wind. Days of it. I sigh, shaking my head. "Oh no."

Addy steps closer, leaning in to see what I'm staring at. Her arm lightly brushes against mine, and I almost forget what I'm looking at for a second. "What is it?" she asks, her voice quiet but anxious.

"It's looking like it's going to last a few days," I say, trying to keep my tone even, but there's no sugarcoating it.

Her eyes widen in disbelief, a hint of panic creeping in. "A few days? But Christmas is in three days!" She bites her lip, her hands fidgeting as if she's trying to hold back a wave of emotion. For a second, I think she's about to cry. Her face softens, and her eyes gloss over with unshed tears, adding to the storm brewing outside.

Maybe she really is scared about missing Christmas with her family. Or maybe she's a fantastic actress, putting on a performance worthy of an Oscar. Either way, I can't deny that she's convincing.

I let out a slow breath, trying to gauge her reaction. "We'll figure it out," I offer, keeping my eyes on her. "For now, we've got plenty of food, warmth, and shelter. We'll make do."

She blinks, her expression torn between gratitude and worry. "Thank you, Travis. I really appreciate you letting me stay here."

I study her for a moment longer, trying to decide if she's really in over her head or playing me like a violin. Either way, the storm outside is very real, and we're both stuck here.

I plate up two dishes, the smell of garlic and herbs filling the warm cabin, and we move to the dining room. The low glow of the fire casts soft shadows over the table, adding to the cozy atmosphere. I set the plates down and glance at her as she eagerly digs in.

"How is it?" I ask, trying to sound casual, but part of me really wants to know if she likes it.

She closes her eyes and lets out a soft, appreciative moan as she takes another bite, her expression one of pure satisfaction. "It's so good," she says, her voice almost reverent. "I didn't realize how hungry I was until I took my first bite."

Her words trigger an unexpected swell of pride. I've cooked this dish countless times, but there's something different about hearing her praise. Something satisfying about seeing her enjoy it after the long day we've both had.

I watch her for a moment longer, the way her cheeks flush slightly from the warmth, how she twirls the pasta around her fork with a natural ease. The soft glow of the fire reflects in her eyes, and it makes her look even more at home, despite the circumstances.

I take a bite of my own, nodding. "I'm glad you like it," I say, trying to keep things light, but there's a part of me that can't shake the feeling that I'm letting my guard down. Just a little.

She catches me staring and smiles, her lips curving up in a way that's both genuine and infectious. "You're a good cook, Travis. I'm impressed."

I shrug, but inside, her compliment lands deeper than I expect. "I've had some practice," I reply, trying to stay casual, but the tension I've been holding starts to ease, if only for the moment.

Chapter 5

Addy

I can't shake the feeling that Travis doesn't trust me, like he's watching my every move, waiting for me to slip up. I mean, I guess I can't really blame him. If I were in his shoes, having some random woman stranded at my cabin in the middle of nowhere just before Christmas, I'd probably be on edge too. But still, the tension is there, unspoken, lingering between us.

As I sit at the table, eating the pasta he made, I sneak a glance at him. His jaw is tight, his eyes flicker toward me, but there's a distance—like he's waiting for something. I wonder if it's more than just general wariness. Maybe he's the type of guy who prefers to be left alone. He certainly has that rugged, mountain-man vibe going on, like someone who's used to his own company.

I twirl some more pasta around my fork, trying not to feel too awkward, but the silence between us feels heavy. I can't help but think about how weird this situation is. I'm in some stranger's cabin, with a snowstorm raging outside, and Christmas is only a few days away. I was supposed to be in Florida by now, sitting on the beach with my family, sipping hot cocoa and laughing at old holiday movies.

Instead, I'm here. With him.

He glances at me again, and I catch his eye this time. "You okay?" he asks, his voice gruff but not unfriendly.

I nod, forcing a smile. "Yeah, just thinking about how strange this all is. I wasn't exactly planning on spending Christmas like this."

His gaze softens slightly, but there's still that guarded look behind his eyes. "Yeah, well, life has a way of throwing curveballs," he mutters, like he knows that all too well.

I can tell there's more to him than just the stoic, reserved man sitting across from me. But I'm not sure if he's the kind of guy who lets people in. Maybe that's why he doesn't trust me—because he doesn't trust anyone easily.

I try to push the thoughts away and focus on the food. "This pasta's amazing," I say, hoping to ease some of the tension. "You really didn't have to go through all this trouble for me."

He shrugs like it's nothing, but I don't miss the way his lips twitch, almost like a smile is threatening to break through. "It's no trouble," he says, but there's something in his tone that tells me he's not used to cooking for anyone but himself.

I take another bite, trying to figure him out. There's a part of me that wants to break through that wall he's got up, to get him to trust me, to relax. But for now, I guess I'll just have to take things slow.

"No Christmas tree?" I ask, glancing around his cabin.

The place is cozy and well-kept, but there's not a single hint of holiday cheer. No lights, no stockings, and definitely no tree. Just the crackle of the fire and the rustic charm of his wooden furniture.

He shrugs, leaning back in his chair. "Nah. Wasn't really expecting company."

I raise an eyebrow, trying to inject some levity into the heavy atmosphere between us. "Oh, come on, it could be fun decorating a tree. Don't you have any decorations lying around?"

His lips press into a thin line, and he looks almost uncomfortable, like the idea of putting up a Christmas tree is somehow foreign to him. "I might have a few in the attic," he mutters, like he's not entirely sure and not entirely thrilled with the idea.

I perk up, feeling a spark of excitement. "Well, why not? It's Christmas, after all. What's a cabin in the snow without a tree? We could make it look festive in here. Maybe it'll even put you in the holiday spirit."

He looks at me, and for a moment, I think he might say no, that he's perfectly fine with his plain, undecorated space. But then something shifts in his expression—just a flicker of curiosity or maybe nostalgia.

"I haven't put up a tree in years," he admits, his voice low, as if he's revealing a secret he doesn't share often. His eyes seem to wander off, like he's remembering something distant, something bittersweet.

I smile softly, trying to nudge him without pushing too hard. "Well, there's a first time for everything. Or in your case, maybe a second or third. Let's make this cabin a little more Christmassy. I'll even help bring everything down from the attic."

He lets out a small sigh, but I can tell he's starting to relent. "I guess we could see what's up there," he finally says, though his tone is still uncertain, like he's not entirely sure what he's getting himself into.

"Great!" I grin, already imagining stringing lights and hanging ornaments. This could be fun—a way to make this strange, snowbound Christmas a little brighter for both of us. Maybe decorating a tree together will chip away at some of that guardedness he's got. Maybe, just maybe, he'll start to warm up to me.

As he stands to head toward the attic, I catch a glimpse of something softer in his eyes, like the idea of Christmas, of the joy and memories it brings, isn't completely lost on him.

Travis heads to the attic, and I follow, trying to suppress a giggle. I can't help but think how odd this situation is being snowed in with a rugged stranger in the middle of nowhere, convincing him to decorate for Christmas like it's a Hallmark movie waiting to happen.

He pulls down the rickety ladder with a creak, dust flying off the edges. "I can't promise anything great is up here," he warns, his gruffness not exactly instilling confidence.

"Hey, we're working with what we've got," I say cheerfully, climbing up after him. "Besides, it's not about having the perfect decorations. It's about the spirit of it, you know?"

He gives me a sidelong glance. "Right. The 'spirit.'"

The attic is musty and cluttered, with random boxes and old furniture shoved into corners. Travis shuffles through a pile of mismatched items, and after some rummaging, he pulls out a dusty box marked "Christmas Stuff" in faded black marker.

"Found it," he says, holding it up like he just discovered a treasure map.

I lean over, peeking inside as he opens it. "Ooh, let's

see what you've got." The first thing I spot is a tangled mess of Christmas lights. They're ancient, the kind with those huge colored bulbs that look like they belong in a vintage postcard. "Wow. These are... retro," I say, holding them up like a tangled web of holiday chaos. "Do they even work?"

Travis raises an eyebrow. "No idea. Haven't used them in forever."

I start untangling them, only to get hopelessly tangled myself. "Uh, little help here?" I laugh as I try to shake free from the lights that seem to have a life of their own, wrapping around my arms like a snake.

He chuckles—actually chuckles—as he steps over to help. "You're a mess."

"Hey, you're the one with the ancient lights," I fire back, grinning as he tries to unwind me. His hands brush against mine as he works, and for a split second, I feel a weird jolt of electricity—not from the lights, but from him.

He clears his throat and steps back once I'm free. "Okay, let's see if these things actually work."

We drag the box downstairs, and once we plug the lights in, there's a loud pop and a flash of light. The whole string flickers once, twice, and then... darkness.

"Whoa!" I yelp, jumping back. "I think we just blew a fuse."

Travis smirks. "Told you they were old."

I shake my head, laughing despite myself. "Okay, so maybe the lights are a bust. But what about the ornaments?" I dig through the box and pull out a few. There's a mix of random, weird stuff—a wooden reindeer missing a leg, a lopsided angel made of what looks like corn husks, and a bright red ball ornament with "Merry Christmas 1996" written in glitter.

I hold up the red ball. "Seriously? This is your idea of Christmas spirit?"

He shrugs. "It's what I've got."

"Well," I say, still smiling, "we'll make it work."

We set up a scraggly pine tree he'd already chopped down and brought inside earlier, and I climb up on a chair to start hanging the ornaments. But as I stretch to place the wobbly angel on top, I lose my balance.

"Whoa!" I wobble, arms flailing, when suddenly Travis grabs me around the waist to steady me. His hands are firm, strong, and way too close to my sides, making me acutely aware of how close we are.

"You okay?" he asks, his voice low, his grip still steady on me.

I nod, breathless for reasons that have nothing to do with almost falling off the chair. "Yeah, thanks. Maybe you should handle the angel."

He smirks and reaches up, easily placing the crooked angel on top of the tree. "See? No need for all the drama," he teases, his eyes glinting with amusement.

"Hey, I'm just adding a little excitement to the evening," I say, hopping off the chair. "Besides, what's decorating a tree without a near-death experience?"

Travis actually laughs, a deep rumble that catches me off guard. It's the first real laugh I've heard from him all night, and it makes me smile even wider. Maybe this whole "grumpy mountain man" thing is just an act.

"Well," he says, stepping back to admire our handiwork, "it's not the prettiest tree, but I guess it'll do."

I glance at the tree—it's lopsided, with a mishmash of strange ornaments and a broken angel teetering on top. But somehow, it's perfect.

Chapter 6

Travis

What is happening to me? Seriously. This woman is like a walking ball of chaos and Christmas cheer, and somehow, I'm letting her pull me into it. I haven't even thought about decorating for Christmas in years—let alone let anyone in my space like this. But here I am, standing in my cabin, with a lopsided tree and a stranger who's turned my life upside down in less than a day.

I watch her as she fusses with one of the ornaments, her brow furrowed in concentration. She's got this way about her, like she's not afraid to dive into things headfirst —even if it's a tangled mess of lights or a scraggly tree. There's something magnetic about it. Something that's drawing me in despite every instinct screaming at me to keep my distance.

She glances over her shoulder at me and catches me

staring. "What?" she asks, her voice light and teasing. "You look like you're contemplating life over there."

I shake my head, snapping myself out of whatever trance I was in. "Just thinking how you managed to turn this place into a Christmas explosion in under an hour."

She laughs, the sound soft and genuine. "I've got a talent for holiday chaos. You should see my bakery this time of year. It's like a gingerbread house exploded inside."

I find myself smiling again. *What is wrong with me?* I don't smile like this. I don't laugh at strangers' jokes. I sure as hell don't invite them to decorate my cabin. But something about her... it's like she's wedged herself into my space and my mind, and I can't shake her loose.

"So, Travis," she says, placing the last ornament—a tiny red stocking—on a low branch. "You gonna tell me what's got you hiding up in the mountains like a hermit?"

I blink, caught off guard by the question. "I'm not hiding," I say, a little too quickly. "I like my privacy."

She smirks, crossing her arms. "Mmhmm. That sounds like hiding to me."

I narrow my eyes, leaning against the back of the couch. "You really like pushing people, don't you?"

She shrugs, a playful glint in her eye. "Only when they need a little push. And you, Mr. Mountain Man, seem like you could use a shove."

I chuckle, despite myself. "You're something else, Addy."

She beams at the compliment, and something inside me softens. It's been so long since I've let anyone in. I've been so focused on my work, on my plans, that I haven't even thought about what it might be like to let someone share my space—even if it's temporary.

"So, what's the plan now?" she asks, plopping down on the couch and pulling a blanket over her lap. "Are we just going to ride out the storm and wait for Christmas to magically arrive?"

I shrug, sitting down across from her. "Pretty much. The storm's getting worse. Roads'll be closed for a few days, at least."

Her face falls for a second, but she quickly covers it with a forced smile. "Well, looks like you're stuck with me, then."

I don't know why, but the thought of her being here for a few more days doesn't bother me as much as it should. Maybe it's the warmth she's brought into this place, or maybe it's the way she lights up the room with that infectious smile. Either way, I can't deny that something about having her here feels... right.

"Could be worse," I say, my voice low, almost to myself.

She looks at me, eyebrows raised. "What was that?"

I clear my throat, standing up and moving toward the kitchen. "I said, it could be worse. You could be a terrible cook or bad company."

She laughs, and it's like a burst of warmth in the cabin. "I'm glad I passed the test, then."

I grab two mugs from the cupboard and pour us both some hot chocolate. When I hand hers over, our fingers brush, and I feel that same jolt from earlier. She takes the mug with a smile, but I can't shake the feeling that there's something more happening here. Something I didn't plan for.

And I don't know if that's a good thing or not.

"We can watch a Christmas movie," Addy suggests, her voice light and hopeful, like the idea of cozying up with some holiday cheer might fix everything.

I glance over at her, still flipping the fuses in the electrical box like a madman, as if somehow doing it over and over will make a difference. "Power's out," I tell her, my voice gruff with frustration. "I don't know if it's the storm, or from when we tried to plug in those ancient lights. Either way, we won't be watching anything anytime soon."

She moves to the window, pressing her forehead lightly against the frosted glass as she stares out at the swirling storm. The snow is relentless, hammering the cabin and piling up against the porch like a force of nature determined to lock us inside. "This is horrible," she whispers, her breath fogging the window.

I pause, feeling the weight of her disappointment, even though she tries to keep it light. It's not just the power going out. It's the whole situation. Stuck in a stranger's cabin, missing Christmas with her family, no idea when she'll be able to leave. I can see the thoughts swirling in her head just like the snow outside.

"It's not ideal," I admit, leaning against the doorframe of the utility room. "But we've got food, a fire, and a roof over our heads. It could be worse."

She turns around, folding her arms over her chest, the blanket she was wrapped in still draped over her shoulders. "I know, I know. I'm just… I don't know. I'm a Christmas person, okay? The movies, the decorations, the baking—it's all my thing. I had this whole vision of what it was going to be like, and now…"

She trails off, biting her lip. I get it. Hell, I used to be the same way. Christmas meant something more back when I wasn't isolated up here, running from my past and drowning in work.

I take a step closer to her. "It doesn't have to be perfect, you know."

She raises an eyebrow, a small smirk tugging at her lips. "Oh, and I suppose you're the expert on Christmas?"

I shrug, leaning against the back of the couch. "Not lately, no. But I've learned a thing or two about expectations."

She laughs, and it's a soft, warm sound that fills the room in a way the Christmas lights couldn't. "Okay, wise mountain man, what's your plan for salvaging this Christmas?"

I look around, scratching the back of my neck. "Well, without power, we're kind of limited, but..." I gesture toward the fireplace. "We've got a fire. We can make s'mores, drink more hot chocolate. Pretend we're on some kind of Christmas camping trip."

Addy's eyes light up a little at the idea, and she seems to relax. "S'mores by the fire, huh? That actually doesn't sound terrible."

"See? Not the end of the world." I give her a lopsided grin. "And if we're lucky, maybe the power will come back before we run out of marshmallows."

She pulls the blanket tighter around herself, that same playful glint returning to her eyes. "Alright, Travis, I'm in. Let's do Christmas, storm style."

I head toward the kitchen to gather supplies, but not before stealing one last glance at her. There's something about her—something that's breaking through the icy walls I've spent years building. And for the first time in a long time, I'm not sure I want to stop it.

Chapter 7

Addy

"Just like this," Travis says, demonstrating how to remove the perfectly toasted marshmallow from the stick and sandwich it between the graham crackers and chocolate. His movements are so deliberate, like everything he does, a sort of careful precision that I'm starting to associate with him. "And now," he adds, holding up the gooey creation like it's a masterpiece, "you have a s'more."

I giggle, feeling a little silly and warm inside. "So easy," I reply, mimicking his technique but with far less finesse. The marshmallow sticks to my fingers, and I end up with more of it on my hands than between the crackers. "Or not."

He chuckles, the deep sound of it blending with the crackle of the fire. "It's all about patience." His eyes twinkle slightly, making me wonder if he's talking about more than just the marshmallow.

I fumble with my sticky creation, trying to keep it from falling apart. "Well, patience isn't exactly my strong suit. Especially when it comes to desserts."

Travis leans back, watching me with a smirk playing on his lips. "I would've guessed that."

I glance over at him, narrowing my eyes playfully. "Oh, really? And what gave that away, Mr. Marshmallow Master?"

He grins, biting into his own s'more with practiced ease. "Just a hunch."

The firelight flickers between us, casting shadows on the rustic wooden walls of his cabin. The storm outside rages on, but in here, by the fire, it feels strangely peaceful. Like we've created this little bubble of warmth, away from the world. I take a messy bite of my s'more, marshmallow oozing out from the sides and sticking to my lips.

"Okay, maybe I see the appeal now," I mumble, trying to catch the runaway marshmallow before it gets worse. "These are amazing."

Travis watches me for a second, his gaze lingering a bit too long, and I feel a blush creep up my cheeks. His eyes are soft, not the guarded, suspicious look he had when we first met. There's something warmer in them now, like he's letting his walls down—just a little.

"You've got a little…" He gestures to his own lips, and I realize too late that I've got marshmallow smeared across mine.

"Oh, great," I mutter, trying to wipe it off with the back of my hand. Of course, now I just look ridiculous, smearing it more.

Travis laughs again, but this time it's softer, almost tender. Without thinking, he leans forward, grabbing a napkin from the side table, and gently wipes away the mess from my face. His fingers brush against my skin for just a second, but it sends a jolt of warmth through me that has nothing to do with the fire.

"There," he says, his voice a little quieter. "All clean."

I blink, not sure what to say, because the sudden closeness between us is unexpected but not unwelcome. The way his eyes lock onto mine makes my heart skip a beat, and for a moment, I forget about the storm, the power outage, and the fact that we're two complete strangers thrown together by circumstance. It feels like something more than that.

"Thanks," I whisper, my voice barely above a breath.

He leans back, breaking the tension with a small smile, and gestures toward the fire. "So... Christmas with a tree, and we've got s'mores. What else do you usually do?"

I laugh softly, feeling the tension ease again. "Oh, you know, the usual. Watch Christmas movies, bake cookies, sing off-key carols with my family. Pretty standard stuff."

He raises an eyebrow. "Sing, huh? You any good?"

"Not even a little," I admit with a grin. "But that's half the fun."

Travis shakes his head with a smirk. "I don't sing."

"Oh, come on," I tease, nudging him with my elbow. "Everyone sings at Christmas. It's like a rule or something."

"I'm pretty sure I can get through the holiday without it," he says, his voice low but teasing.

I lean back, looking at him curiously. "You must have some Christmas traditions, though. Something you do up here, all alone on the mountain?"

He shrugs, glancing away like he's not sure how to answer. "Used to be different. Spent Christmas with my family. But... things change."

There's a weight to his words, a heaviness I didn't expect, and it makes me pause. I want to ask more, to dig a little deeper, but I also don't want to push. Whatever it is that's keeping him up here in this cabin, isolated from the world, feels personal.

"I get that," I say softly, taking another bite of my s'more. "Christmas has always been a big deal for my family. It's weird not being with them right now."

He looks at me then, really looks at me, and there's a flicker of something in his expression—understanding, maybe. "Must be hard, being stuck here."

I shrug, trying to lighten the mood. "Could be worse. I mean, I'm stuck in a cozy cabin with a fire, s'mores, and... well, you." I flash him a teasing smile.

He laughs, a real one this time, and it lights up his whole face. "Guess that's not the worst way to spend Christmas."

The storm howls outside, but in here, everything feels strangely right. And as I sit next to Travis, our shoulders just barely touching, I realize that maybe this Christmas, as unplanned and unexpected as it is, might just be one I'll never forget.

Chapter 8

Travis

Every cell in my body vibrates with the need to kiss her. The firelight flickers against the walls, casting a soft glow over her face. She's sitting just inches away, smiling at me with those big, bright eyes, and I can't stop staring. The way her lips curve up in that playful grin, the way her hair falls just so across her shoulders—it's like everything around us has faded away, leaving just her.

The storm outside continues to rage, snow battering the windows, but in here, it's warm. Cozy. Intimate. Almost too intimate.

I don't know what it is about Addy, but she's got me all twisted up inside. At first, I kept telling myself she could be part of some scheme Mayfair cooked up. That old fox could have hired her to get close to me, spy on what I've been working on. But now... I don't care. Honestly, I don't. Whether Mayfair sent her or not, all I know is that

I'm sitting here with a beautiful woman, and every rational thought I had is slipping away, replaced by one simple truth: I want to kiss her.

Her laughter lingers in the air as she finishes the last bite of her s'more, the marshmallow sticking to her lips again. I catch myself staring at her mouth, unable to look away, the urge to lean in stronger than ever.

She brushes the crumbs off her hands, completely oblivious to the war I'm fighting inside myself. "You're staring," she says with a soft laugh, meeting my gaze.

"I know," I admit, my voice low. I don't even bother denying it. How could I? The truth is written all over my face.

Her smile falters just a little, her eyes searching mine like she's trying to figure me out. "What?" she asks softly.

What do I say? That I've never felt this kind of pull before? That I've spent years alone, thinking I'd be fine without anyone to share my life with, and now, suddenly, she's here and everything feels different?

I lean in slightly, just enough to see the flicker of surprise in her eyes, but I stop myself, clenching my jaw. "I don't think I've had company like this in a long time," I say, which is probably the understatement of the century.

She raises an eyebrow, tilting her head. "How long?"

I lean back slightly, running a hand through my hair, trying to break the tension before I do something stupid. "Too long."

The words hang between us, heavy and full of meaning. She shifts, tucking a strand of hair behind her ear, suddenly looking a little nervous herself.

"I guess I could say the same," she murmurs, her gaze falling to the fire. "I wasn't expecting to be here, but... it's not so bad."

I let out a soft chuckle. "Not so bad, huh?"

She grins, her eyes meeting mine again. "Well, you did save me from freezing to death in the snow. That earns you some points."

Her playful tone eases some of the tension, and I find myself laughing, shaking my head. "I'll take that." But the moment of levity fades as quickly as it came, and my gaze drifts back to her lips. The fire crackles, filling the silence between us, but it's not enough to drown out the thoughts racing through my mind.

I could kiss her right now. I want to. Every part of me is screaming to close the distance between us, to feel her lips on mine, to see if this pull between us is as real as it feels.

I shift a little closer, watching her reaction. She doesn't move away. Her breathing seems to quicken just a fraction, and I see the way her gaze flickers to my mouth. It's like she's waiting for it, expecting it, maybe even wanting it as much as I do.

And that's all the encouragement I need.

"Addy..." Her name slips from my lips in a whisper, and it sounds more like a confession than anything else. I'm not sure what I'm about to say, but the moment is broken by a loud gust of wind battering the window, making the whole cabin groan.

She flinches slightly, pulling her attention back to the storm, and the moment's lost.

I curse silently, leaning back and running a hand over my face. What am I doing? This is insane. I barely know her. For all I know, she could still be working with Mayfair, and here I am, practically ready to kiss her like I'm some lovesick idiot.

"Looks like we'll be snowed in for a while," I mutter, trying to regain some sense of control. "Hope you're not in a rush to get anywhere."

She laughs lightly, her eyes still flicking back to me now and then. "Well, I was planning on getting to Florida by Christmas, but I guess the universe had other plans."

I grunt in response, trying not to focus too much on the fact that she's sitting just inches away, or how easily I could close the gap between us. "Guess so."

But even as I say it, I know the truth. This—whatever is happening here—it's more than just the storm, more than some freak accident that led her to my cabin. There's something about her that I can't shake, something that makes me feel alive again in a way I haven't felt in years.

She looks back at me, her gaze soft, her lips parting like she wants to say something. But before she can speak, I lean forward just slightly, my voice low and rough. "Addy, if I kiss you right now…"

Her breath hitches, and for a second, everything freezes. The fire crackles, the wind howls, but we're both locked in this moment, waiting.

"I wouldn't stop you," she whispers.

And that's it. Every doubt, every question about Mayfair and whatever scheme I thought she might be a part of disappears. There's only her, and the pull between us that I can't ignore any longer.

I close the distance, my hand coming up to cup her cheek as I press my lips to hers. It's soft at first, tentative, but the second I feel her respond, the kiss deepens. All the tension from earlier, all the unspoken things between us, it all comes pouring out in that kiss.

And suddenly, I know—this woman is going to change everything.

Chapter 9

Addy

The warmth of Travis's kiss envelops me, melting away the cold that's seeped into my bones from hours in the storm. The fire crackles softly in the background, its light dancing across the walls, adding a soft glow to the already intimate atmosphere.

For a moment, the rest of the world ceases to exist. There's only the feeling of his lips on mine, the steady rhythm of his heartbeat against my chest, and the undeniable connection that seems to spark and crackle with every touch.

When we finally pull away, breathless and slightly dazed, Travis's eyes hold mine with an intensity that makes my heart race. The room feels charged, electric, and I can't help but notice how the warm light highlights the sharp angles of his face, the way his dark hair falls just right, and the way his eyes are so full of... everything.

"I didn't expect that," I whisper, my voice still trembling from the kiss and the lingering cold.

"Neither did I," he admits, his voice a low rumble that seems to vibrate through me. "But it felt right."

I nod, feeling a smile tugging at my lips. "It did."

The moment is interrupted by a loud thud outside, followed by a gust of wind that shakes the windows. The storm is still raging, a constant reminder that we're stuck here together, isolated from the rest of the world.

"I guess we should make the best of it," I say, trying to lighten the mood. "How about we finish decorating that Christmas tree? I'd hate for it to go without its fair share of tinsel and ornaments."

Travis's lips curl into a small, amused smile. "You really want to decorate the tree?"

"Why not? It's Christmas, after all," I reply with a playful grin. "Plus, it's better than just sitting here in the dark."

He chuckles softly, shaking his head in disbelief. "Alright, let's do it. But don't expect me to be a pro at this."

We head back to the living room, where the half-decorated tree stands, its branches weighed down by a few ornaments and a bit of tinsel. I can't help but laugh as I take in the sight—Travis's idea of decorating seems to involve a lot of improvisation.

I reach for a box of decorations and start pulling out the glittery baubles and garlands. Travis joins me, trying to untangle a particularly stubborn strand of lights.

"You know," I say as I hang a shiny red ornament on a branch, "I didn't expect to end up here, in the middle of a storm, decorating a tree with a handsome stranger."

He looks up from the tangled lights, his brow furrowing slightly. "No?"

I shake my head, laughing softly. "Nope. But sometimes, the best moments are the ones you don't plan for."

Travis raises an eyebrow, a smirk playing at his lips. "You're quite the optimist, aren't you?"

"Guilty as charged," I say, flashing him a bright smile. "And you're not so bad yourself."

As we continue to decorate, the conversation flows easily between us. We talk about everything from our favorite Christmas traditions to the strangest things we've ever eaten. I learn that Travis is surprisingly passionate about cooking, that he's a stickler for detail, and that he values his privacy fiercely.

I, in turn, share stories about my bakery, Addy's Sweet Treats, and the mishaps that have happened over the years. Travis listens intently, his eyes never leaving mine, and I find myself feeling more at ease with him than I've ever felt with anyone.

The tree is finally looking festive, adorned with tinsel, ornaments, and a sparkling star on top. We step back to admire our work, the soft glow of the lights reflecting off the decorations.

"It looks great," I say, feeling a sense of accomplishment.

"It does," Travis agrees, his gaze lingering on me. "Thanks for convincing me to do this."

I glance around the room, taking in the cozy, festive atmosphere. "Thanks for letting me be a part of it."

He nods, his expression thoughtful. "So, what's your plan now?"

I bite my lip, feeling a bit uncertain. "I guess I'll just have to wait out the storm. I hope the power comes back on soon so I can call my parents and let them know I'm okay."

Travis looks thoughtful for a moment before speaking.

"If the storm keeps up, it might be a while. But we'll make do. It's not so bad, right?"

I smile, feeling a warmth that goes beyond the fire. "Not bad at all. In fact, I'm starting to think this might be one of the best Christmases I've had in a long time."

Travis looks at me with a mixture of surprise and something else—something that looks a lot like hope. "Yeah? Even with all this chaos?"

I nod, taking a step closer to him. "Even with the chaos. Sometimes, it's the unexpected moments that turn out to be the most memorable."

He meets my gaze, his eyes softening. "I think you might be right about that."

As we stand there, the storm howling outside and the fire crackling in the hearth, I realize that, despite everything, I wouldn't trade this moment for anything. The storm might be keeping us here, but it's also brought us closer together. And for now, that's more than enough.

The evening stretches on, filled with laughter, stories, and a growing sense of connection that neither of us expected. The storm rages on outside, but inside, the warmth of the fire and the closeness of each other make it feel like Christmas came early.

Chapter 10

Travis

The morning light filters softly through the cabin's windows, casting a gentle glow over the room. I lie awake, staring at the ceiling, my thoughts tangled and restless. Last night was unexpected in so many ways—Addy's presence, the warmth we shared, the connection that seemed to grow with every passing hour. I hadn't planned on falling for anyone, especially not during a storm that kept us isolated from the world. But here I am, grappling with feelings I thought I'd buried long ago.

Addy's peaceful breathing from the other side of the room is a soothing soundtrack. She's curled up under a cozy blanket on the sofa, looking more serene than I've seen anyone in a long time. There's a part of me that wants to stay here, just like this, forgetting about everything else. But I know I can't.

I slip out of bed and head to the kitchen, trying to

shake off the disquiet in my gut. The storm outside has lessened, but the cold is still biting. I start a pot of coffee, hoping the strong aroma will help clear my mind.

As I wait for the coffee to brew, my phone buzzes on the counter. It's Jackson. I hesitate for a moment before answering, knowing that if there's any update on the situation, he'll have it.

"Hey, Travis," Jackson's voice comes through the line, sounding unusually grave. "I've got news. We've confirmed it—Mayfair did indeed plant a spy. It's part of his latest scheme. He's been trying to gather intel on your work and any upcoming projects."

My heart skips a beat. I try to keep my voice steady. "Are you sure about this?"

"Positive," Jackson replies. "We traced it back to one of his operatives. It's definitely someone working for him. I wanted to let you know so you can be on alert. Be careful."

The weight of his words hits me hard. My mind races, trying to connect the dots. The strange behavior, the way Addy seemed almost too perfect for this situation—could she really be the spy?

I glance over at the sofa where Addy is still sleeping, her face soft and innocent. The thought of her being involved in something like this feels like a punch to the gut. But Jackson's information doesn't lie. Mayfair is a ruthless businessman, and he wouldn't hesitate to use any means necessary to get what he wants.

I take a deep breath, trying to steady my emotions. The coffee pot gurgles to life, filling the cabin with its rich aroma. I need to think clearly, assess the situation, and figure out the best course of action. I can't let my personal feelings cloud my judgment.

After ending the call with Jackson, I try to calm my racing thoughts. I make a pot of coffee, hoping it will provide some clarity. But as I stir the coffee, my gaze keeps drifting back to Addy. I don't want to believe she's involved in anything nefarious. But if Mayfair is behind this, and she's working for him, it's my responsibility to protect myself and my work.

The morning stretches on, and I find myself wrestling with a mix of betrayal and confusion. I need to confront Addy, find out if she's been honest with me. But I also need to be careful—accusing her without proof could destroy whatever trust we've built in these few short days.

As I sip my coffee, the realization hits me hard. I need to be on high alert, not just for my own safety, but for the feelings I'm starting to develop for her. If she is a spy, I'll need to navigate this carefully—both for my own protection and for the growing emotions that are tangled up in this mess.

I look out the window, the morning light casting long shadows on the snow. The storm may have passed, but the real challenge is just beginning.

Chapter 11

Addy

I wake up to the smell of coffee and the muted sounds of a storm that has finally started to quiet down. For a moment, everything feels perfect—the soft, warm blanket wrapped around me, the aroma of freshly brewed coffee, and the comforting sound of Travis moving around the kitchen. I stretch and slowly get up, feeling the pleasant warmth of the cabin against the lingering chill from the night before.

As I make my way to the kitchen, I see Travis at the counter, his back turned to me. His shoulders are tense, and there's a furrow in his brow that wasn't there last night. My heart sinks a little, noticing the change in his demeanor. Last night was wonderful; we shared moments that felt so genuine. But now, something feels off.

"Good morning," I say, trying to sound cheerful as I approach him.

He turns to face me, his expression unreadable. "Morning."

I pour myself a cup of coffee, trying to gauge his mood. The warmth of the coffee cup in my hands is soothing, but it doesn't dispel the unease that's creeping up my spine. I take a sip, savoring the taste and trying to collect my thoughts. I'm still thinking about how I'm going to get to Florida, the storm's impact on my plans, and what I need to do next.

Just as I'm about to ask Travis if he has any idea when the roads might clear, he speaks, his voice tinged with an edge I've never heard before.

"So, you're a spy for Mayfair?"

The coffee nearly spills from my hand as I freeze, my heart skipping a beat. "What? What are you talking about?" I manage to stammer, trying to process his words.

"I know about the scheme," he says, his gaze hardening. "Jackson confirmed that Mayfair planted a spy. And you're the only stranger I've had in my cabin."

The accusation hits me like a cold slap. My stomach churns, and I feel a wave of confusion and hurt wash over me. "Are you serious?" I ask, my voice trembling. "Why would you think that? I came here because my car broke down. I told you I was on my way to visit my parents."

"Yeah, well, that's what a spy would say," Travis retorts. "You show up right when I'm isolated by a storm. It's too convenient."

I feel my cheeks flush with a mix of embarrassment and anger. "You think I'm here to spy on you? I was just trying to get to my family for Christmas!"

The accusation stings deeply, and I can't stand the thought of being mistrusted, especially after the bond we seemed to build. My hands shake as I put my coffee cup down on the counter. "You know what? Maybe it's better if I leave."

I don't wait for his response. Without another word, I grab my bags and head for the door. The cold air slaps me in the face as I step outside, the snow crunching underfoot. I can barely see through the frosted windshield of my car, but I make my way to it with a determined stride.

As I get in and start the engine, my breath fogs up the windows. The car sputters to life, and I try to ignore the stinging tears in my eyes. The road is still snow-covered, but I have to try. I need to get away from this place, away from the hurtful accusations and the man who I thought might have been different.

As I drive away from the cabin, the snowflakes swirling around me, I can't help but feel a pang of regret. I wanted this to be a Christmas to remember for the right reasons, but instead, it's become a chaotic mess. The road ahead is uncertain, and the only thing I know for sure is that I need to clear my mind and get as far from this place as I can.

Chapter 12

Travis

The morning is bleak and overcast, the storm having left a thick blanket of snow over everything. I'm pacing the cabin, my mind a whirlwind of confusion and regret. I just accused Addy of being a spy for Mayfair, and now she's stormed out, leaving me with nothing but a growing sense of guilt and frustration.

I grab my phone and dial Jackson's number, my hands shaking slightly. When he picks up, I waste no time.

"Jackson, I need to know something. Who's the spy for Mayfair?"

"Travis? What's going on?" Jackson's voice is laced with concern.

"Just answer the question. Who's the spy?"

There's a brief pause, and then Jackson speaks. "It's not Addy."

The words hit me like a punch to the gut. I feel the

color drain from my face. "What do you mean it's not Addy?"

Jackson explains, "The spy's supposed to be someone else. Addy's just a regular person. I double-checked with my sources after your call."

I feel a mix of anger and shame as I absorb the news. I've been wrong about Addy—about everything. The realization stings worse than the cold outside.

Without another word, I hang up and rush to my truck, my boots crunching on the snow as I move. I need to find her, make things right, and apologize for the way I treated her. My hands grip the steering wheel tightly as I speed down the road, my mind racing with the possibility of losing her forever.

The drive is tense and nerve-wracking. Snowflakes whip around my truck as I push the vehicle to its limits, navigating the treacherous roads with a single focus—finding Addy before it's too late.

As I approach Snowflake Village, the small town is beginning to come to life, the early morning light casting a soft glow on the snow-covered streets. I scan the surroundings desperately, my eyes darting from one side of the road to the other.

When I finally see her car parked outside the Sweet Brew coffee shop, my heart leaps into my throat. I pull over, throwing the truck into park, and make my way toward her vehicle. The sight of her car, and the thought that I might still have a chance to make amends, propels me forward.

I walk briskly to the coffee shop, pushing through the door with determination. The warm, cozy aroma of coffee fills the air, and I spot Addy sitting at a corner table by the window. Her posture is slumped, and she looks lost in thought. The sight of her like this, looking so vulnerable and alone, only intensifies my regret.

"Addy," I call out, my voice firm but filled with desperation. "Please, wait. I need to talk to you."

She looks up, her eyes widening with surprise and something else—pain, maybe. I approach her slowly, my heart pounding in my chest. I take a deep breath, struggling to find the right words.

"I'm so sorry," I start, my voice breaking slightly. "I was wrong about you. Jackson confirmed that you're not the spy. I shouldn't have accused you."

Addy's gaze softens, but there's still a hint of hurt in her eyes. "So, you finally believe me?"

"Yes," I say, feeling a weight lift off my shoulders. "I do. And I'm sorry for everything. I was just... I was trying to protect myself and my work. But that doesn't excuse how I treated you."

She nods slowly, her expression conflicted. "I wanted to be honest with you, Travis. I was just trying to get to my family for Christmas. I never meant to cause any trouble."

I feel a pang of guilt as I realize the impact of my actions. "I know. And I should have trusted you. I just... I let my fears get the best of me."

I reach out, hoping she can see how sincere I am. "Can we start over? I'd like to make it up to you, if you'll let me."

Addy's gaze lingers on me for a moment, and then she finally offers a tentative smile. "Okay. Let's talk. But first, I think we both could use a cup of coffee."

We sit together at the table, the warmth of the coffee shop enveloping us. As we talk, I can't help but feel hopeful. The storm outside may have caused chaos, but maybe, just maybe, we can find a way to clear the skies between us.

Chapter 13

Addy

The aroma of freshly brewed coffee and the hum of casual chatter create a comforting backdrop as I sit across from Travis at the Sweet Brew coffee shop. I stir my coffee absently, my mind replaying the recent events with a mix of disbelief and relief. Travis's apology was unexpected, but it was exactly what I needed to hear.

He takes a deep breath, his gaze meeting mine with a sincerity that makes my heart ache. "Addy," he begins, his voice steady but soft, "I need to explain why I jumped to conclusions about you."

I nod, encouraging him to continue. "Go ahead."

Travis runs a hand through his hair, a gesture that reveals his frustration and vulnerability. "I thought you were a spy hired by Mayfair. Jackson, my brother, told me that the spy was supposed to be someone else. I should have trusted you more. I was wrong to accuse you."

His confession hangs in the air between us, and I can see the genuine remorse in his eyes. My own heart begins to thaw from the frost of yesterday's confrontation.

"I never wanted to cause you any trouble," I say quietly. "I was just trying to get to my family for Christmas. I didn't expect any of this."

He reaches across the table, his hand brushing against mine. The touch is warm and reassuring, a tangible reminder of his sincerity. "I know. And I'm really sorry. I was just so wrapped up in my own worries and the pressure of my work that I didn't see what was right in front of me. I let my fears get in the way."

I squeeze his hand gently, appreciating the gesture. "Thank you for coming after me. It means a lot."

A shy smile tugs at the corners of his lips. "I didn't want to lose you. Even if it started out on the wrong foot, I've really enjoyed getting to know you. And I'm not ready for this to end."

My heart skips a beat at his words. "Neither am I."

We share a smile that seems to bridge the gap between us, a silent agreement that we both want to move forward. The storm outside continues to rage, but inside, it feels as though the clouds are clearing.

"So, what now?" I ask, my voice soft but hopeful.

Travis looks thoughtful for a moment before his expression brightens. "Well, since we're snowed in for a few days, how about we make the most of it? We could start by finishing decorating the tree and then maybe do something fun together. I'd really like to get to know you better."

I nod, feeling a surge of excitement at the prospect. "That sounds wonderful. I'd love that."

We spend the next few hours working together, decorating the tree with a mix of laughter and playful banter. The old lights that didn't work earlier now shine brightly, and the cabin feels even more like home with each ornament we hang. We find comfort in each other's company, sharing stories and dreams as the snow continues to fall outside.

As evening falls, we sit by the fire, the warmth of the flames and the glow of the Christmas lights creating a cozy, intimate setting. Travis looks at me with a tenderness that makes my heart swell.

"I'm really glad we got this chance," he says, his voice filled with emotion. "I never expected to find someone like you."

I smile, feeling a deep sense of contentment. "Me neither. But I'm grateful that we did."

We share a quiet moment, the connection between us growing stronger with each passing second. As we sit together, I can't help but feel that this unexpected turn of events has led us to something truly special.

The storm outside may be fierce, but inside the cabin, surrounded by the warmth of the fire and the twinkling lights of the Christmas tree, everything feels just right. I lean into Travis, and as he wraps his arm around me, I know that we've found something rare and precious.

In the midst of the snowstorm and the chaos, we've found our own little piece of happiness. And as I look at Travis, I'm filled with hope for the future—a future that, despite the unexpected beginning, feels incredibly bright and full of promise.

Epilogue

Addy

The snow-covered landscape of Snowflake Village glistens under the bright morning sun, casting a serene glow over the quaint town. The storm has finally passed, leaving behind a winter wonderland that looks like it's straight out of a storybook. As I look out the window of the cozy cabin where Travis and I have spent the last few days, I can't help but smile at the thought of how much has changed.

Travis is in the kitchen, putting the final touches on breakfast. The aroma of fresh coffee and sizzling bacon fills the air, mixing with the sweet scent of the cinnamon rolls I baked earlier. It's become a bit of a routine for us to cook together, and each meal feels like a celebration of the connection we've found.

I'm still amazed at how things have unfolded. After the storm, Travis and I spent our days decorating the cabin, making the most of our time together. We laughed, talked, and shared dreams by the fire, and as the days passed, our bond grew stronger. It wasn't long before I realized that I was falling for him—hard.

My phone buzzes on the counter, pulling me out of my thoughts. I glance at it and see a text from my parents checking in to see if I'm safe and asking when I'll be arriving. It's a reminder that, despite everything, my journey to Florida is still ahead of me.

Travis comes into the room, carrying a tray of breakfast. He sets it down on the table and looks at me with a warm smile. "Ready for breakfast?"

I nod, returning his smile. "Absolutely. I've never been so excited for a meal."

As we sit down to eat, I can't help but reflect on how much has changed since that fateful night when my car broke down. What started as a chance encounter with a rugged, mysterious man has turned into something truly special. The way Travis looks at me, the way he cares for me—it all feels like a dream come true.

"So, what's next for you?" Travis asks, his eyes sparkling with curiosity.

I take a moment to savor the question. "Well, I'm definitely looking forward to getting back to my bakery in Cresthaven. But I'm also excited about the future. I think... I think I'd like to see where this goes with us."

Travis reaches across the table, taking my hand in his. "Me too. I can't imagine my life without you now. I know we have a lot to figure out, but I'm willing to take that journey with you."

We share a moment of quiet understanding, the weight of our words settling between us. It's a promise—a promise to explore the future together, no matter where it leads.

After breakfast, we pack up the last of our things and get ready to head back to Cresthaven. As I look around the cabin one last time, I feel a pang of sadness at leaving this magical place, but I'm also filled with excitement for what's to come.

As Travis and I drive away, the beauty of the snow-covered mountains fades into the distance, but the warmth in my heart stays with me. The road to Florida is still ahead, but with Travis by my side, I feel ready to face whatever comes next.

I glance at him, catching his eye with a smile. "Here's to new beginnings."

He smiles back, his hand finding mine. "Here's to us."

And as we drive towards the future, I know that no matter what challenges we may face, we have each other. And that, more than anything, makes me feel like we've found our own little piece of forever.

About the Author

Em Tate is an emerging author of sweet holiday romances. She loves all things Christmas, and may one day branch out into the world of small town romances.
Em promises in each book you'll find…

Clean and Wholesome characters.
PG content.
Enemies-to-Lovers
And a Happily-Ever-After

Come join Em Tate's reader group over on Facebook, CLICK HERE!

Also by Em Tate

The Snowflake Village Series
Snowflakes and Second Chances
Tinsel and Twirls
Mistletoe and Magic Wishes
Sleigh Bells and Sweethearts
Peppermint and Candy Canes

Mistletoe Kisses Multi-Author Collaboration
A Husband For Christmas

Made in the USA
Monee, IL
15 December 2024